x793.8 B78h

Broekel, Ray.

Hocus pocus

HOCUS POCUS:
MAGIC YOU CAN DO

Ray Broekel and Laurence B. White, Jr.

Illustrated by Mary Thelen

ALBERT WHITMAN & COMPANY, CHICAGO

EVANSTON PUBLIC LIBRARY
CHILDREN'S DEPARTMENT
1703 ORRINGTON AVENUE
EVANSTON, ILLINOIS 60201

*This book is dedicated to our friend
Steve Dusheck, who invents more tricks
than most magicians perform.*

Text © 1984 by Ray Broekel and Laurence B. White, Jr.
Illustrations © 1984 by Mary Thelen
Published simultaneously in Canada by
General Publishing, Limited, Toronto
All rights reserved. Lithographed in the U.S.A.

Library of Congress Cataloging in Publication Data

Broekel, Ray.
  Hocus Pocus.

  Summary: Step-by-step instructions for twenty simple
magic tricks, together with tips on patter, timing,
sleight-of-hand, and misdirection for the beginning
magician.
  1. Tricks—Juvenile literature. 2. Conjuring—
Juvenile literature. [1. Magic tricks] I. White,
Laurence B. II. Thelen, Mary, ill. III. Title.
GV1548.B72 1984   793.8   83-26096
ISBN 0-8075-3350-5

  12 11 10 9 8 7 6 5 4 3

CONTENTS

GETTING
STARTED

THIS IS A HARE-RAISING
EXPERIENCE...
BY THE WAY, I CALL MY
RABBIT HARRY, BECAUSE
HE HAS SO MUCH FUR!

You can learn how to do the tricks in this book, but that won't make you a magician. To be a magician, you must know more than how a trick works. You must know how to entertain people. Good magicians keep their audiences fooled and entertained by using a number of important tools.

Patter—what a magician says—is one of the most important. Imagine two different magicians who do the same trick. The first says, "Ladies and Gentlemen, I will tear this newspaper into tiny pieces . . . Then I will say the magic word ABRACADABRA . . . Notice that the newspaper is back in one piece!"

The second magician does exactly the same thing, in exactly the same way, but he has given more thought to his patter:

Ladies and Gentlemen, I have a really TEAR-*able trick to show you . . . Do you realize how weird paper is? You rip it* UP *by tearing it* DOWN. *You know, it's funny but my dog gets spanked if he tears up the newspaper, and here I am getting applause for it. Applause, please?*

And now, with the help of a mighty, mystical incantation GOOEY, GOOEY, SOFT AND CHEWY, *the paper has mysteriously mended itself. Or has it? Maybe it was never really torn in the first place.*

Which of these magicians would you rather watch? The first one is just doing a trick. The second is a showman. If you plan and practice your patter before you perform, you will be a better magician.

Timing—doing or saying exactly the right thing at exactly the right time—is another important magician's tool. It requires lots of practice. In the trick "X Marks the What?" (pages 40-41), a red card with an X and a yellow card are put into an envelope. When they are taken out, the X appears to have jumped from the red card to the yellow one. If you present the trick well, the audience will suspect there is a third card hidden in the envelope. There isn't. You could just open the envelope to show them, but with timing, you can have a lot more fun.

Pretend the audience has caught you, act embarrassed, tease them. Look inside the envelope yourself and say, "No, I told you there is nothing in there." Your audience will probably scream to see. Then hold the envelope open so one person can see inside. Say, "Do you see anything in there?" Whisper loudly, "Say NO!" By now if your timing has been right, people will be absolutely sure there is an extra card inside. Suddenly tear open the envelope and show that it is empty. To entertain and fool an audience, magic must be done at exactly the right speed and patter must be presented in exactly the right places.

Many tricks are self-working. They require no special skill, just the ability to do one thing after another in the

MY DOG GETS SPANKED
WHEN HE DOES THIS —
BUT I GET PAID FOR IT!

MY WAND IS MADE FROM
THE WOOD OF THE
SILENT DOGWOOD TREE.
THAT'S THE TREE WITH
NO BARK!

correct order. "A Pack of Kings and Aces" (pages 20-21) is such a trick. But sleight of hand tricks rely on a performer's skill with his hands to make magical things happen. Sleight of hand is still another important magician's tool. A magician's term for a secret action is *sleight* (slīt). One common sleight is a *palm*. When you palm an object, you keep it hidden in your hand. The trick "One Plus One Equals Three" (pages 42-43) uses a special kind of palm called a "finger clip." Other tricks using sleights are "Stick 'Em Up!" (pages 22-23), "Knot Me!" (pages 26-27), "The Left-Handed Knot" (pages 38-39), and "Color Magnets" (pages 44-45).

Good magicians also know how to use gimmicks. Gimmicks are special pieces of equipment that make a trick work but are unknown to the audience. In "The Mystery of Canada" (pages 32-33), the gimmick is a magnet. As long as you keep the magnet a secret, no one will guess how you do the trick. Gimmicks must be your greatest secret.

Misdirection is the magician's most important tool. It is making people look where you want them to. Suppose you are palming a paper ball in your right hand and don't want your audience to look closely at that hand. You hold your right hand still and point with your left hand to some balls on the table. "I will use these two paper balls for my trick," you say. People will look at the balls on the table. That's misdirection. People will look where you look, point, or tell them to look. Misdirecting your audience takes a surprising amount of practice. Doing "One Plus One Equals Three" will help you practice misdirection.

Practice is what sets a magician apart from people who just "do a trick or two." Sometimes it helps to practice the various parts of a trick separately, before putting them all together to do the entire trick. For example, you might first do "One Plus One Equals Three" without the extra palmed ball. Just use two balls and pretend to end with three. Then when you add the extra ball, the trick won't be too difficult. Your misdirection should be perfect. Practice means doing a trick more than a few times. Practice alone, in front of a mirror, or in front of friends. Only after lots of practice can you hope to be a real magician.

DO YOU KNOW HOW to MAKE A RABBIT FLOAT? JUST MIX TWO SCOOPS OF ICE CREAM WITH CLUB SODA AND ONE RABBIT!

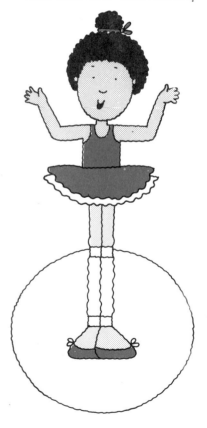

THE INVISIBLE MACHINE

The Trick

You ask a person to clasp her hands together and squeeze tightly. The squeezing is important.

As she is holding her hands in that position, you reach into your pocket and pretend to bring something out. "This," you explain (showing nothing), "is my invisible machine. You'll notice that it has a screw on each side." You point to two places about four inches apart. Of course, there is nothing to see.

"Let me show you how my machine works," you say. "Keep your hands clasped together but stick out your two pointing fingers and hold them about an inch apart."

When the person has done this, you pretend to place the invisible machine on top of her fingers. Be careful not to touch the fingers yourself.

"Now watch what happens when I tighten the screws." You put one of your hands on each side of the extended fingers and begin to twist as though you were tightening invisible screws.

Even *you* will be amazed to see the extended fingers slowly and mysteriously move toward each other as if some invisible force were pushing them together.

Here's How

It's amazing! This trick works itself. Try it with your own hands right now. Just clasp them together tightly for a minute, then extend your two pointing fingers while keeping your other fingers interlocked. Hold the tips of the pointing fingers about one inch apart and wait a few seconds. They will move toward each other on their own, very quickly. The feeling is uncanny.

You take advantage of this strange fact by pretending that your "invisible machine" is responsible. If you practice a few times with a friend you will learn how to time your moves so you can start "tightening the screws" just as the fingers begin to move together. If your timing is right, many people will believe *you* are actually pushing the fingers together.

FOR tHIS tRICK i NEED tHE HELP OF A KIND PERSON — ANY KIND!

THE CARD THAT WHISPERS

The Trick

Shuffle a deck of cards and show the faces to your audience. "Notice the cards are all different and well mixed," you say. You set the deck face down on a table between you and a helper. Then you cut the cards and place half the deck in front of your helper. Ask him to pick up the card you cut to but not to let you see it.

You pick up the top card from the other half of the deck. "This card," you explain as you hold the card up to your ear, "will whisper the name of the card that you are now holding."

You pretend to listen for a moment. Then you name the card your helper is holding! And just to prove it was not a lucky guess, you repeat the same trick again and again. (But not too many times. You don't want to bore people!)

Here's How

After you fan out the cards so the spectators can see the faces, take a quick look at the top card and remember it. Set the deck face down on the table near you. Cut the cards and place the *top* half in front of your helper. Ask him to take the "card you cut to" and look at it. (It really isn't the card you cut to. It is the top card of the deck—the one you remember.)

Then take the top card from the bottom half of the deck (the half nearer you) and hold it up to your ear so you can hear it "whisper." Of course, it can't really whisper. You just say this so you can see the face of the card as you move it up to your ear. (Don't stare at it so people will notice. Just glance at it quickly, making sure to remember what it is.)

Then pretend the card whispers the name of your helper's card. You already know what it is so you are only acting. But your helper will be surprised.

To do the trick again, simply drop the card you are holding (which you now know) on top of the cards in front of you. Ask your helper to return his card to the stack in front of him. Now drop your cards on top of his stack. The new card you know is on top of the deck. You are all set. You can do the trick over and over as long as you put the whispering card back on top of the deck each time and remember what it is.

SOME PEOPLE THINK HE'S FAR AND AWAY the BEST MAGICIAN. I THINK HE'S BEST WHEN HE'S FAR AND AWAY!

PENNY MIND READING

The Trick

Hand a number of pennies to a helper. Then turn your back to him and say, "So I will not know how many pennies we will be using, would you remove any number from 0 to 5 and set them aside? We will use only the pennies you keep. I will not know how many that is."

After the helper does this, you say, "Count to yourself the number you have left and take away pennies to represent that number. If you have 11 pennies, take away 1 and 1, or 2 pennies, and set them aside. If you have 16 pennies, set 1 and 6 aside."

When this is done, your back should still be turned to your helper. "Now," you say, "from the pennies you have left, keep any number you wish and hand the rest to me. Hide the pennies you keep in your fist."

Your helper hands you some pennies behind your back. You feel them and turn around to face him. "By feel I can tell you have given me 4 pennies," you say, "and by magic I can tell that you are hiding 5 pennies!"

He is! And you can immediately repeat the trick and all the numbers will be different.

Here's How

Begin with exactly 19 pennies. Ask your helper to discard any number from 0 to 5. At this point you honestly do not know how many pennies he has left.

Next you ask him to count the remaining coins and discard a number "to represent that number." This step is the key that lets you do the trick. Remember your helper had 19 pennies to begin with and discarded no more than 5. This means he must be holding between 14 and 19 pennies.

If he holds 14, he discards 1 and 4, or 5 pennies.
If he holds 15, he discards 1 and 5, or 6 pennies.
If he holds 16, he discards 1 and 6, or 7 pennies.
If he holds 18, he discards 1 and 8, or 9 pennies.
If he holds 19, he discards 1 and 9, or 10 pennies.

In every case he will be left with nine pennies! So now you do know how many pennies he has.

To finish the trick, have your helper keep some of the pennies and hand you the rest. Simply subtract the number you are given from 9 and you know how many he has hidden in his fist.

You can repeat the trick once or twice, but don't repeat it too many times or someone will catch on!

tHis tRick is fOOLPROOf, AND i'M just tHe fOOL to PROve it!

AMAZING ACES

i tried this trick on the t.v. last night, but i failed because i fell off!

The Trick

Show a deck of cards to a helper. "Somewhere in this deck are the four aces," you explain. "I would like you to find them for me even though you have no idea where they are . . . Numerologists believe that numbers have magical properties. Let's see whether they do. Please give me any number between 10 and 20."

Suppose the person names 14. You count 14 cards off the deck and put them in a pile. Picking up the pile, you explain, "In numerology, the number 14 is made of a 1 and a 4. Added together they make 5. Let's see what the fifth card in this packet is." You count off 4 cards and flip over the fifth. It is an ace!

Putting the packet back on the deck, you invite another person to be your helper. Suppose he gives you the number 19. You count off 19 cards, add 1 to 9 to give 10, count 9 cards off the packet, and flip over the tenth. It is another ace!

Repeat the pattern two more times with two different numbers, and the two remaining aces will turn up!

Here's How

This is a puzzling mathematical trick. It will amaze even you. Take the four aces and set them on top of the deck. Then take any nine cards from the bottom of the deck and set them on top of the aces. Now you are ready.

Just repeat the following actions four times and an ace will automatically appear each time. Ask someone to give you a number *between* 10 and 20 (not 10 or 20). If the person names 14, count 14 cards onto the table one at a time from the top of the deck. Put each card on top of the one just counted. Count aloud as you set the cards down. Stop at 14. Set the rest of the deck to one side and use the counted packet for the next step.

Add the two digits of the number together. With the number 14, add 1 and 4 to get 5. Count off this number from the top of the packet, again setting each card on top of the card just counted. Turn over the fifth card and it will be an ace. Toss the ace face up in the middle of the table and leave it there.

Now pick up the cards you just counted (keeping them face down) and set them UNDER the cards in your hand. Then set this packet on top of the cards you set to one side. It is important to restack the cards in just this way. Now you are ready to do the trick again. You can repeat the pattern three more times. Practice counting out the cards and restacking them until you can do it without thinking. This may become your favorite card trick.

THE LADY THAT FLOATS IN THE AIR

The Trick

"All great magicians float beautiful ladies in the air," you explain while searching through a deck of cards. Removing a single card, you go on, "I will now teach you to do this difficult trick. I will use a beautiful lady . . . the Queen of Hearts."

You hold the card between your fingertips so people can see the face. "The secret is to say the magic words 'your ROYAL HIGHNESS, will you please rise?'"

You remove your fingertips and the card seems to float in the air. Then it starts to rise. When it has reached your head, you quickly grab it and pull it down. "My, our royal highness certainly is lightheaded this afternoon, isn't she?" you say.

Here's How

The trick is simple but it does take practice. Do it before a mirror until you've mastered it. You need only a small piece of tape that's sticky on both sides. For practice you can use a piece of well-chewed gum, but the tape works best.

To begin, stick the piece of tape on the tip of one of your thumbs. Have the deck of cards handy. To find the Queen, spread the cards out, face up, on a table. You do not want the tape to touch the cards, so handle the deck and the Queen with your other hand.

When you locate the Queen, pick the card up and hold it between your outstretched fingertips. Press your taped thumbtip against the back of the card as you show the audience the face. Keep your thumb in this position.

When you want the card to "float," *slowly* move your fingertips away from the sides. Your thumb is hidden behind the card and your hands will appear not to be touching it.

To cause the card to float upward, simply move your two hands up, with the fingers around, but not touching, the sides. The card will appear to float inside your spread fingertips. Move your hands faster and faster to make it look as if the card is trying to get away. When it reaches your head, grab it with your fingers and pull it down. Take your thumb away (be sure the tape comes with it) and you are left with an ordinary card that can go right back into the deck. Pick up the deck with the same hand that has the taped thumb and drop it into your pocket. When the hand is inside the pocket, just scrape off the tape and leave it there. No evidence of your mystery will be discovered!

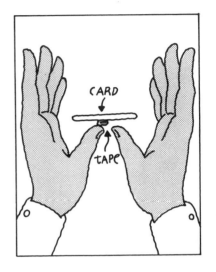

HOW TO BE HOUDINI

The Trick

"Today I would like to try one of Houdini's most famous escapes," you explain as you show a thick pole and two pieces of rope. "The trick is called 'The Wooden Handcuffs.' The pole will hold my hands so far apart they won't be able to come together to untie the knots."

You lay the bar across your shoulders and grasp each end with a hand. Ask two friends to come forward. Each takes a rope and ties one of your wrists to the bar. You say, "It took Houdini about a half hour to untie himself. I will do it in five minutes. Please time me."

Someone in the audience looks at a watch. You step out of sight for about thirty seconds and return holding the ropes and the bar.

Here's How

The props are two pieces of soft clothesline, each about eighteen inches long, and a four-foot-long broomstick. Lay the pole across your shoulders and put a hand on each end to hold it in place. This puts your wrists in the proper position for tying.

Ask two people to tie your wrists to the pole but not so tightly it hurts you. The secret is that they can only tie your wrists against the pole. (Your wrists will be parallel to the pole.) When they are done, you can easily slide your wrists *and* the ropes along the pole!

Now you must disappear from view for about thirty seconds. Step into another room or ask your two helpers to hold up a blanket as a screen.

When you are out of sight, twist one of your wrists so you can grasp the bar with one hand. Push that end of the bar toward your head. The bar will slide through the rope on your other wrist. When your grasping hand is just above your shoulder, release your grip and grab the pole with your other hand. Slip the first hand right off the end of the pole. Use your free hand to slide the pole off the other wrist. Without the pole in place, the loops of rope should roll right off your wrists.

Don't bother to untie the knots. That takes too much time. You want to do this trick as fast as you possibly can.

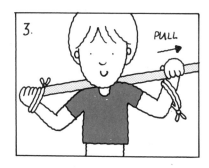

A PACK OF KINGS AND ACES

The Trick

This trick will drive people crazy! You hold a packet of eight cards in your hand. "The packet I'm holding," you explain, "is made of the four kings and the four aces. I have arranged them in a special order that lets me do this trick."

You hold the packet face down in one hand. You take the top card and slip it, still face down, onto the bottom of the packet. You turn the next card face up. It is an ACE, and you lay it on the table.

You repeat the actions, taking the new top card and placing it on the bottom, then turning the next card face up on the table. it is a KING.

You repeat the actions again, putting the top card underneath the packet and the next card face up on the table. It is an ACE.

You continue to repeat the actions until you run out of cards. Finally you will have, face up on the table, ACE-KING-ACE-KING-ACE-KING-ACE-KING.

"That's the trick," you explain as you hand someone in the audience the packet. "Just arrange the cards in the right way so you end up as I did."

The trick sounds and looks simple, but it isn't. People probably won't be able to arrange the cards correctly even if they spend an hour!

Here's How

This trick *is* done by arranging the cards in the correct order, but the order is so unusual very few people ever figure it out.

Ready for the magic formula? From the top of the packet down, arrange the cards in this order:

KING
ACE
ACE
KING
ACE
ACE
KING
KING

Now you're all set. Just put the top card on the bottom of the stack and turn the next card face up. Then repeat the pattern until all the cards are on the table. The kings and the aces will alternate. Remember the arrangement, but keep it our secret!

YOU CERTAINLY ARE THE VERY BEST AUDIENCE I'VE HAD THIS AFTERNOON!

WOW!

STICK 'EM UP!

The Trick

Wrap a length of rope around your hand and elbow. Then suddenly point your forefinger at someone as though you were holding a gun. Say, "Hands up! Do you know what will happen if I shoot this rope at you?"

"No," the person will probably answer.

"KNOT a thing!" you say, flipping the rope off your elbow toward her. "KNOT A THING!"

A knot has appeared in the rope.

Here's How

This is a cute, quick trick. It is not a mysterious marvel. You should do it as quickly as possible so no one will notice how you make the knot form.

The rope you use should be between five and six feet long and *quite* soft. Both the length and softness of the rope are important. If you use clothesline rope, be sure it is cotton and has been soaked overnight in water. The soaking will wash out the starch and make the rope more flexible.

Wrap the rope around your hand and elbow as shown in the middle picture on the next page. Then just flip the loop off your elbow toward the spectator while holding the short end in your hand. The knot will form automatically.

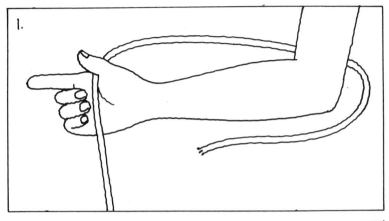

Make one of your hands into a "gun" by pointing your forefinger in front of you and curling the rest of your fingers. Wrap the rope around this hand and elbow. The long end of the rope should run between the thumb and forefinger, in front of the palm, and down toward the floor.

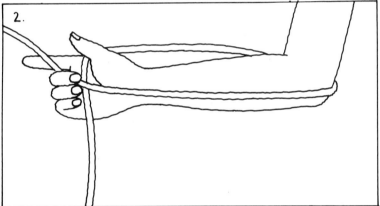

Pinch the rope (near the short end) between your middle finger and palm to hold it in place. Your thumb should stay free.

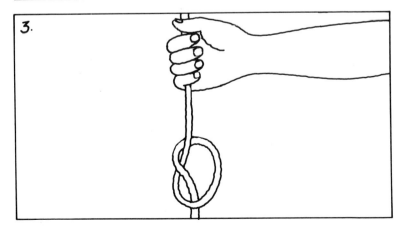

Keeping hold of the short end of the rope, flip the loop off your elbow, toward the audience. A knot should form on its own.

THE CARDS OF OUR CHOICE

The Trick

You look through a deck of cards and remove one. You lay it face down on the table. "I have chosen a card that I like," you say to a helper. "It is one of my favorites. Do you have a favorite card?"

Your helper will probably say yes. You hand her the deck.

"Please take out the card of your choice as I did." When she has done this, you cut the deck and place half face down in front of her. You ask her to place her card on top. When she has, you drop the rest of the deck (except for the card you chose as your favorite) on top.

"So neither of us knows where your card is," you say, "would you cut the deck several times?"

She does this and her card is completely lost. You hand her your card face down. "Please take the card of my choice," you say, "and without looking at it push it into the deck anywhere."

She does. You ask her to cut the deck several more times. You say, "The card of my choice was the three of clubs. What card did you choose?"

"The king of spades," she replies.

You ask her to find the two cards, and she does. Do you know where? Side by side!

WHO'S HE KIDDING?

Here's How

When you first look through the deck, take out *any* card and don't even bother to remember its name. But, as you are looking, do remember the name of the *top* card in the deck. Don't take it. Leave it on top but remember its name. Lay the odd card face down on the table.

Hand the deck to a helper and ask her to look through it and remove the card of her choice. Take the deck back and cut it in half. Set the *top* half of the deck on the table in front of the helper and ask her to drop her card on. Then drop the rest of the pack on top.

You have made your helper drop her card on top of the top card in the pack and you know the name of that card!

Now ask her to cut the deck several times. Only rarely will this upset the order. The two cards will most probably stay together. Next have her put "the card of your choice" (the odd card you removed earlier) into the deck wherever she chooses. And have her cut the deck several times.

Now you name your card. Of course, you really name the card that was on top of the deck.

She names her card and finds both cards side by side!

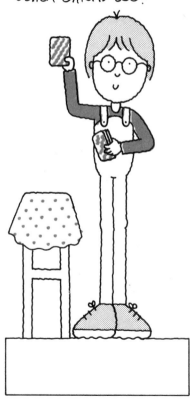

this trick was invented by the world's greatest magician! of course, i've invented a few other tricks too!

KNOT ME!

The Trick

"May I have a little knot music, please?" you ask as you tie a knot in the middle of a piece of rope. "Thank you," you say when you finish. "That certainly was NOT music."

Pointing to the knot you say, "Most people would have to untie this knot to get rid of it, but not a magician."

You wrap your hand around the knot and slowly slide your fist downward. "A magician would simply take the knot off the end of the rope, like this."

Your fist slides off the end of the rope and the knot is gone. "And he would toss the knot to his audience!"

You toss your hand toward the audience and a knot flies out!

Here's How

Take a length of cotton clothesline and soak it overnight in water. This will get rid of the starch and make the rope soft and flexible. Let it dry thoroughly.

Cut off two feet. This will be the piece you show to the audience. Tie a knot near the end of the remaining rope and cut the knot off. Trim the ends of the knot to keep it as small as possible.

Now tie a *loose* knot in the middle of the two-foot-long piece of rope and practice slipping it off the end. (This will automatically untie it.)

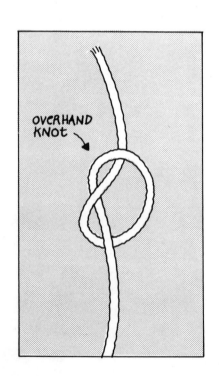

OVERHAND KNOT

The secret is to slip your thumb inside the loop of the knot as you wrap your fingers around it in a fist. If you made the knot loose enough, your thumb will fit easily inside. Your fingers will keep people from seeing your thumb. Now move your fist downward. Your thumb will do all the pulling. The loop of the knot will slip right off the bottom of the rope.

If anyone tries to do this without putting a thumb inside the loop, the knot will simply tighten and stay in the center of the rope.

To perform the trick, just hide the small knot in the hand that will slide the knot the audience sees off the rope. When the knot has been slid off, toss the little knot into the audience. People will be surprised.

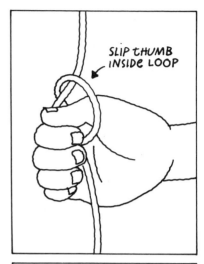

SLIP thUMB INSIDE LOOP

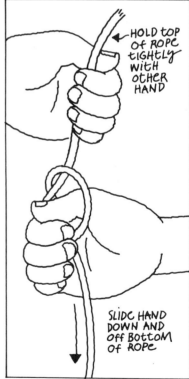

HOLD top of ROPE tightly with other HAND

SLIDE HAND DOWN AND off BOttOM of ROPE

RING OR STRING?

The Trick

As you remove a small loop of string from your pocket you ask for the loan of a finger ring. "Are there any holes in this ring?" you ask, looking for one.

"No," answers the person lending it.

"How about this big one right here," you say, sticking your finger through the ring. "It's the hole you put your finger through, isn't it?"

People will laugh at the joke.

"Now let's find the invisible hole," you go on. You ask the person who loaned you his ring to hold out a finger.

When he does, you thread the loop of string through the ring and hang the ends of the loop over the outstretched finger. Next you lift the ring and slip it over the fingertip.

"Your finger is passing through a big hole we can see, but the string is passing through the invisible hole. I'll prove it. Which do you want, the ring or the string?"

"The ring," the person replies.

"Then I'll just take the string off through the invisible hole," you say, giving the string a little tug. It appears to melt through the ring, which remains on the finger!

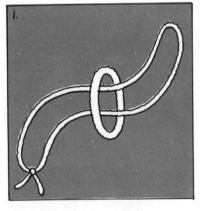

Thread the loop of string through the ring.

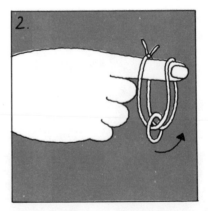

Hang both ends of the loop of string over the helper's finger.

You give the ring to the person and drop the string into your pocket, where it can stay until you do this trick again.

Here's How

Find a twenty-inch piece of heavy, strong string and tie the ends together to make a loop. This and a borrowed ring are all you need.

To do the trick, you must hang the ring on the loop, and the loop on the finger as shown in the pictures. People will think they are linked together. They really are not. Just pull either side of the string on the fingertip side of the ring and the string will pull free.

It doesn't matter whether the person says he would like the ring or the string at the end. If he asks for the ring, take the string and leave him with the ring. If he says he wants the string, simply pull the string free and hand it to him. "Then here it is!" you say. Either way, you still do the same thing. Magicians call this word trick a "magician's choice."

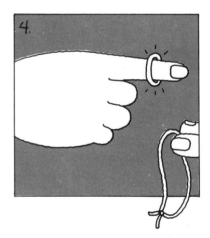

The string will come free and the ring will be left on the finger.

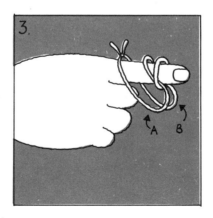

Lift the ring and set it over the tip of the helper's finger. Pull firmly on *A* or *B*.

OUT OF A HAT

HOCUS POCUS!

The Trick

"When I was a small child," you begin, "I saw a magician pull a rabbit out of a hat."

You show both sides of a sheet of newspaper and then begin folding it. "When I got home," you go on, "I did not have a magician's hat so I had to make my own. Of course, it didn't turn out too well. In fact, it looked like this."

You finish folding and display a pointed newspaper hat, which you place on your head. The audience chuckles.

"Also," you continue, "because I was just beginning as a magician I was never able to pull a rabbit out of my newspaper hat. All I could ever find in my hat was a pretty handkerchief like this."

You reach in your hat and draw out a handkerchief (or scarf). "And this one and this one and this one!" Four handkerchiefs! The audience is surprised.

Here's How

This trick works on an old idea. Long ago magicians discovered that you can glue two pieces of paper together to make pockets inside. Flat objects like handkerchiefs can be hidden in these pockets.

To do the trick, just follow the illustrations. Be careful putting the hat on and taking it off. Tip your head forward to meet it so that the handkerchiefs do not fall out. You can use the special paper you made again. For a smaller hat, use a sheet of newspaper folded or cut in half and only one or two handkerchiefs or scarves.

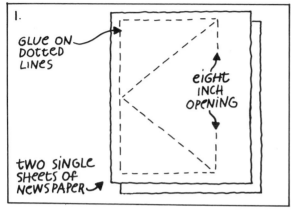

1. GLUE ON DOTTED LINES

eight INCH OPENING

TWO SINGLE SHEETS OF NEWSPAPER

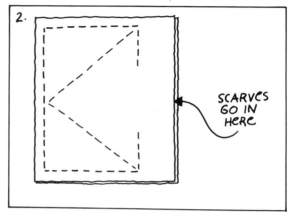

2. SCARVES GO IN HERE

3. NOW it LOOKS LiKE THIS

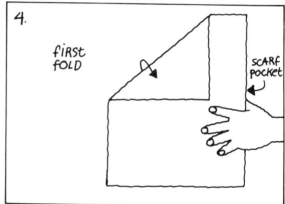

4. FiRST FOLD

SCARf POCKET

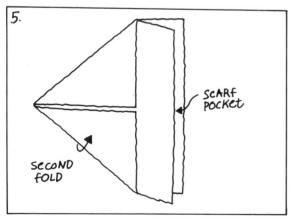

5. SCARf POCKET

SECOND FOLD

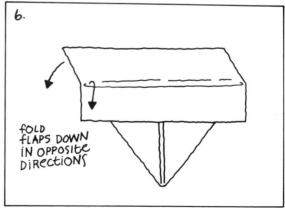

6. FOLD FLAPS DOWN IN OPPOSITE DIRECTIONS

THE MYSTERY OF CANADA

i DID this trick over the RADiO LAst week AND A HUNDRED PEOPLE WROTE IN SAyiNG they DiDN't see HOW i DiD it!

The Trick

"Here are six nickels," you say. "Notice that five are American and one is Canadian." You lay the nickels on a table and cover them with a large scarf. Reaching under the scarf, you mix up the coins.

"Now I challenge you to reach under the scarf and find the Canadian coin just by feel."

People will try but they usually fail.

You remove all the nickels and show a small bottle full of water. Unscrewing the cap, you say, "I will try the same thing but I will make it even harder." You drop the nickels into the jar and screw the cap back on. Then cover the jar with the scarf.

Next you ask a helper to reach under the scarf and shake the bottle to mix up the nickels. When she's finished, you say, "Now I am going to do the impossible. I will remove the single Canadian nickel from the water-filled jar and I will do it without spilling any water!" You reach under the scarf with both hands and begin to manipulate the bottle.

After a minute or two you remove the nickel and toss it on top of the scarf. It is the Canadian nickel! Ask your helper to remove the scarf. The five American nickels will still be in the water-filled jar, and there will be no trace of how you did the trick.

Here's How

A magnet! It is a little-known fact that American nickels are not attracted to a magnet but Canadian nickels are.

You will need a small, wide-mouthed glass jar with a screw-on *metal* cover (like a peanut butter jar), a large scarf nobody can see through, the nickels, and the magnet.

To set up, fill the jar ¾ full of water. Stick the magnet to the underside of the metal cover. (First remove the cardboard liner if the lid has one.) Screw the cover on.

Do the trick just as it's been described. When you reach under the scarf, first turn the jar upside down, then rightside up. The Canadian nickel will stick to the magnet. Then unscrew the cap and remove the nickel and the magnet from the underside of the cap. Screw the cover back in place and remove your hand from under the scarf. As you hold the nickel in plain view, hide the magnet inside your fist. Toss the nickel on the scarf. While everyone is searching for your secret, put your hand in your pocket and leave the magnet there. The audience can search and search but will find nothing more than six nickels, a water-filled jar, and a scarf.

It will take practice to learn how to manipulate the jar under the scarf. Hold onto the jar with one hand. Unscrew the lid and remove the nickel and magnet with your other hand. One final tip—before you drop the nickels into the jar, ask a person to make a pencil mark on the Canadian nickel. That way you can prove it is the same nickel you remove. Just be careful you don't rub off the mark as you handle the coin.

DID YOU GET THAT?

33

LOTS OF THOUGHTS

The Trick

"What would happen if we all thought about exactly the same thing at exactly the same time?" you ask. "Let's do an experiment." You lay a board flat on the table and stand a milk carton in the middle of it. You raise one end of the board to form a hill.

"I will lift this end higher and higher," you say. "When the hill is too steep, the carton will either slide down or fall over. Your thoughts will determine which."

You raise the hill a bit higher and say, "Think about the carton sliding . . . sliding." The carton slides down the hill without falling!

Return the board and carton to the starting position. "This time," you say, "concentrate on the carton falling." You slowly raise the board and the carton falls over.

Do the trick again. The carton will slide or fall depending on what you ask the audience to think about.

Here's How

This "experiment" seems to use ordinary things—a board and a milk carton—but only the board is really ordinary. You'll need *two* cartons, a heavy rock about the size of a golf ball, and some tape and glue in addition to the board. The board should be wider than the milk cartons and about three feet long.

Cut the tops off both cartons and cut the side out of one. Trim this side so it fits into the first carton on a slant. Look at the illustration to see just how to position it.

I.

FALSE SIDE

ROCK GLUED IN FOR WEIGHT

Before fastening the false side, glue or tape the rock to the bottom of the carton as shown (behind the extra side). You may have to experiment with several rocks to find the exact size and weight that will work. The prepared carton will appear empty from the top. But don't let anyone examine it too closely!

The secret is to place the milk carton back on the board after each performance. This gives you a chance to turn the carton so the hidden weight is either toward the top of the hill or the bottom. If the weighted side is toward the bottom, the carton will fall. If the weighted side is toward the top, the carton will slide.

When you're done, say that even you don't know how or why this trick works.

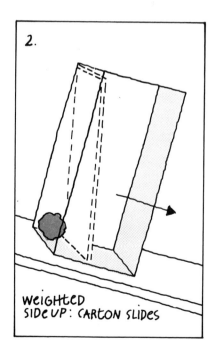

2.

WEIGHTED SIDE UP: CARTON SLIDES

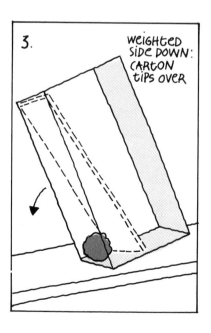

3.

WEIGHTED SIDE DOWN: CARTON TIPS OVER

MYSTICAL MAGIC MONEY

The Trick

On a small cardboard tray you show ten pennies. Say to John and Mary, two helpers from the audience, "These pennies are friends. They like to be together. Let me show you."

You ask Mary to hold out her hand. Then you dump the pennies off the tray into it and ask her to count them out loud as she places them back on the tray. She counts ten pennies. You repeat this with John but ask him to put seven pennies back onto the tray and keep three. He does.

You ask Mary to hold out her hand again and dump in the seven pennies John put back on the tray. Tell her to close her hand around them quickly and tightly. Now take the three pennies from John and drop them into your pocket.

You ask Mary how many pennies she holds. She will answer, "Seven." Then you ask John where the other pennies are. He will say, "In your pocket."

"No, no," you say. "Remember I told you these pennies like to be together. In fact, they cannot be separated."

Standing well away from Mary so no one can suspect trickery, you ask her to count the pennies she holds out loud. "One, two three, four, five, six, seven—" she gasps, "—eight, nine, TEN."

I.

5"

4"

GLUE THREE LAYERS TOGETHER

Here's How

You will need thirteen pennies and a changing money tray. If you want to be extra safe, use only pennies with the same date, though nobody will probably ever check them.

A changing money tray is an ancient magician's prop first used centuries ago. You can make a simple one out of three sheets of 4 x 5 inch cardboard. Glue the sheets together like a sandwich. The middle section must be thicker than a penny and have a cutout section in the center, as shown in the picture.

The tray will hide the three extra pennies inside. If you tip it one way, the hidden coins will stay inside. If you tip it the other way, they will spill out.

To begin, place ten pennies on top of the tray and hide the three extras inside. When Mary holds out her hand the first time, dump the tray so only the ten pennies on top fall into her hand. She counts them out loud as she puts them back onto the tray.

Do the same thing with John. The secret pennies stay inside, and he puts seven back onto the tray.

Then as you turn toward Mary, reverse the tray. Now when you dump the pennies into Mary's hand, the seven on top and the three secret pennies go into her hand. She will not notice because there are so many pennies. Ask her to close her hand quickly and tightly.

Take the three pennies from John and drop them in your pocket. Ask Mary how many pennies she holds. Then proceed to amaze her.

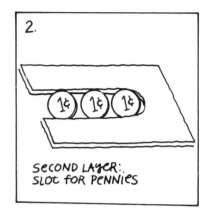

2.

SECOND LAYER:
SLOT FOR PENNIES

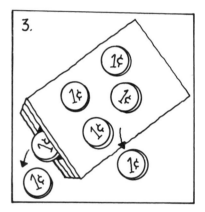

3.

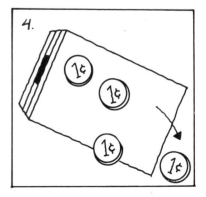

4.

THE LEFT-HANDED KNOT

The Trick

"Do you know the difference between a right-handed knot and a left-handed knot?" you ask, showing a short piece of rope.

"A right-handed knot is tied on my right hand," you explain, holding up your right hand. Loop the rope over your right wrist and pass one end through the loop. When you pull the ends, a knot forms in the rope.

"Right-handed knots are better because they make tight knots," you say. "Left-handed knots are very strange." You untie the knot and loop the rope over your left wrist and again pass one end through the loop. Pull the ends as before—this time no knot forms! "Left-handed knots come untied too easily," you say. "In fact, they untie themselves before they are tied!"

To prove your point, you tie a left-handed knot again, and again no knot forms.

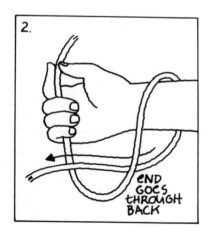

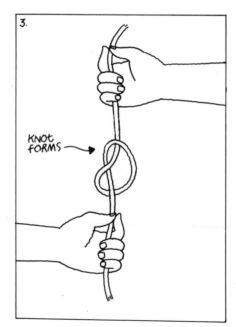

Here's How

The secret, of course, is knowing how to make each kind of "knot." Both are tied almost the same way. But one really is a knot, while the other only looks like one.

Use a soft piece of rope about two feet long. It should be fairly thick so the audience can see it easily. (Cotton clothesline is about right.) To form each knot, just follow the illustrations.

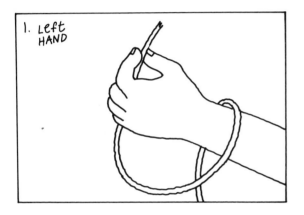

1. LEFT HAND

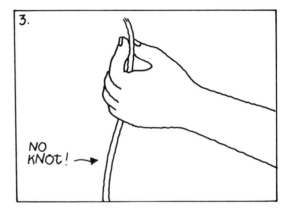

3.

NO KNOT! →

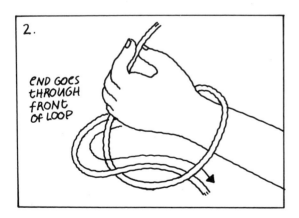

2.

END GOES THROUGH FRONT OF LOOP

"X" MARKS THE WHAT?

The Trick

Take two large pieces of cardboard from an envelope and show them on both sides. One piece is yellow and one is red. Draw a big *X* on one side of the red card. Say, "My job as a magician is to fool you. Your job is not to be fooled. Watch carefully and try not to be fooled."

You show the cards again, then slip them into the envelope. Spin and twist the envelope in front of your audience. "Now," you say, "on which card did I draw the *X*?"

The audience is positive. "Red!"

You slowly withdraw the red card and show it. It is blank on both sides. Then you slowly withdraw the yellow card. It is marked with a big *X*.

The audience is certain there is another card inside the envelope. Reluctantly tear the envelope open. It is empty!

Here's How

As the audience suspects, there are three cards, but they are different from what anyone imagines. One is yellow on both sides, another red, and the third red on one side and yellow on the other. You can make the third card by gluing a red and yellow sheet together. The cards should fit into a large manila envelope.

Take a crayon or marking pen and draw a big *X* on one side of the all-yellow card. Lay the red side of the red-yellow card on top of the *X*. If you pick these two

tHANK you for your APPLAUSE, LADIES AND GENTLEMEN... tHANK you... BOtH of you!

cards up together, they will look like a single yellow card. (Draw a ¼ inch black edge around all the cards. Then if they don't line up exactly, no one will be able to tell.) Now set the plain red card on top of the other two and slip them all into the envelope.

To perform the trick, reach into the envelope and remove the all-red card. Show it on both sides. Next remove the all-yellow and red-yellow cards, squeezing them together so they look like a single yellow card. You'll have to practice to do this convincingly.

Show the double card, then slip it back inside the envelope. Pick up the plain red card and draw an X on it that matches the X you drew earlier on the all-yellow card. (It might help to draw a light pencil X on the card when you are preparing to do the trick.)

Now slip the red card back into the envelope, but be sure to put the side with the X *on top of* the yellow side of the red-yellow card.

Ask the audience, "Which card has the X?"

The answer will be, "Red."

Remove the all-red card and the red-yellow card, squeezing them together to look like a single red card. The X on the red card and the yellow side of the secret card are hidden inside this "sandwich." Only a single yellow card with an X remains in the envelope. Remove it and show it to the audience. The people will be convinced that the red card with the X is still inside. It isn't. Tease them. Then tear the envelope apart and watch their faces drop!

HE'S INCREDIBLE!

41

ONE PLUS ONE EQUALS THREE

these are my two micro-miniature rabbit helpers. this is BUGS ...AND THIS is MABEL.

OH, SURE... AND I'M DUMBO the ELEPHANT!

The Trick

"Let's have a magical math lesson using my two miniature rabbit helpers," you say. "I forgot to bring any real rabbits, so you will have to use your imagination."

Taking a piece of paper, you tear off two small corners and roll them into pea-sized balls. You pick one up and place it in your empty palm. "This is Bugs." You put the second one next to him. "And this is Mabel."

You dump them from hand to hand and point to each of them. "Remember this one is Bugs and that one is Mabel." You dump them back and forth again. "Or is this one Mabel and that one Bugs?" As you dump the balls, you get more and more confused about which is which. Finally you close your fist around them.

"Oh, well, it doesn't matter. Bugs and Mabel were just going to help me with a math lesson. This is it—how many rabbits am I holding?"

"Two," people reply.

"Right!" you exclaim as you open your hand. Everyone is surprised. You are holding *three* paper balls. "Oh, I guess we all forgot about Billy, their bouncing baby bunny!"

Here's How

Before doing the trick, make one extra paper ball the size and shape of the two you will make in front of the audience. Place it and a small piece of paper in your pants pocket.

To do the trick, take out the piece of paper. Hold it up, tear off two corners, and roll the corners into tiny balls.

Put the rest of the paper back into your pocket. Before taking your hand out of your pocket, clip the extra ball between your middle two fingers. Look at the pictures to see how this is done. Curl your fingers around the clipped ball to hide it. Then use the fingers and thumb of this hand to pick up "Mabel and Bugs" and drop them into your other hand. Clip one of these loose balls between the middle fingers of that hand.

You now have a ball clipped in each hand and one ball that is free. The audience sees only two balls resting on your outstretched hand.

Now for some sleight of hand. You appear to dump two balls from one hand into the other, but actually only the free ball goes into the other hand. The other two are always fingerclipped. As you dump the free ball from hand to hand, turn over your dumping hand. The back of the hand will hide the fingerclipped ball. Although you actually show all three balls, you show only two at once. Talking about your two rabbit helpers, Mabel and Bugs, will help trick the audience into believing you have only two balls.

Finally, toss the two balls from one hand into the other so all three are in the same hand. Close this hand immediately into a fist. You are ready to perform your "math-a-magic"!

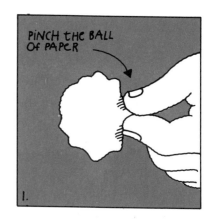

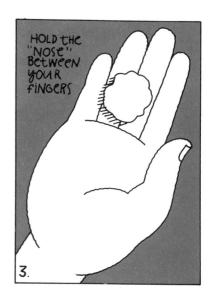

COLOR MAGNETS

The Trick

Hold up two pieces of colored paper, one red and one blue. Tear them each in half. Then roll half of the blue paper and half of the red into two small balls.

Show two empty paper cups and set them on the table, open end up. Pick up the blue paper ball in one hand and the other half of the blue paper in the other. Drop the blue ball and the piece of blue paper into one of the cups. Then drop the red ball and the piece of red paper into the other cup. Now reach into a cup with each hand and remove the flat pieces of paper. Show the slips of paper on both sides.

"Because the balls in the cups were made from these papers," you say, "the papers attract them the way a magnet attracts metal." Cross your arms and let the pieces of colored paper flutter down into the cups (the opposite of the cups they were in before). You appear to watch the balls moving from cup to cup. Of course, nobody else sees anything. Finally, you announce, "They made it!" You ask someone to empty the cups. The blue ball and blue paper are together in one cup, the red ball and the red paper in the other.

Here's How

You'll need two small paper cups, two small pieces of red paper, a small piece of blue paper, and a costume with at least two large pockets. Ahead of time, make a ball from one of the pieces of red paper. (It should match the small red ball you make during your performance.) Put the ball and the two cups in your pockets.

Begin the trick by making a red ball and a blue ball. Set them beside their matching colored papers on the table. Now remove the cups from your pockets. While doing this, palm, or hide, the extra red ball in the palm of one hand. Keep your fingers curled to hide it. (The cup will also block it from view.) You'll need to practice to gain skill in palming.

Show the empty cups, then set them on the table. Pick up the blue ball in the hand with the hidden red ball. Pretend to drop the blue ball into one of the cups, but really drop in the red one. Now hide the blue ball in your hand. Drop the blue paper into the same cup. The audience will think you have put a blue ball and blue piece of paper into the cup. Pick up the red ball from the table. Pretend to drop it into the other cup, but drop in the hidden *blue* ball instead. Palm the red ball. Drop the red slip of paper into this cup. Everyone will think the red ball and paper are together.

With your hands curled into fists (to keep the red ball hidden), reach into each cup with your thumb and forefinger and remove the papers. Be sure people see that you have just removed the papers, not the balls. Cross your arms and drop the papers into the wrong cups (the audience will *think* they are the wrong cups). As someone checks the contents of each cup, casually place your hands in your pockets and leave the secret ball.

I WILL ROLL THESE PAPERS INTO A BALL. AS I DO, MAY I HAVE A LITTLE BUTTER? AFTER ALL — WHAT'S A ROLL WITHOUT BUTTER?

FLOWER POWER

The Trick

"I'd like to give you a lesson in 'Flower Power,'" you explain as you display a stem with leaves and a colorful flower on top.

You pick the flower and slip it into your pocket. Next you drape a handkerchief over the top of the stem.

Say, "When I count to three, shout 'Flower Power' as loud as you can."

You count "One, two, three." The audience shouts, "Flower Power!" You pretend not to hear and count again. "Flower Power!" they shout, louder. You whisk away the handkerchief, but the stem is still flowerless.

"Can't you shout any louder?" you ask, putting the handkerchief back over the stem. The audience screams, "FLOWER POWER!" This time you toss the handkerchief off and there is a flower on top of the stem.

Here's How

This is an impressive trick, but it requires work. Once made, though, the props are always ready for use.

You will need heavy green construction paper, tape, two identical bright-colored plastic flowers with wire stems, a rubber band, a button, green leaves of plastic or cloth, a pencil, and scissors.

First make the flower stem. Wrap the construction paper around a pencil to make a stiff tube. Fasten the edge with tape and slip it off the pencil. Tape a few small leaves to it so it looks like a flower stalk.

HOCUS POCUS!

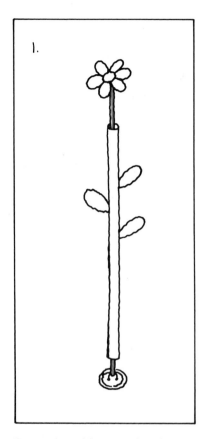

1.

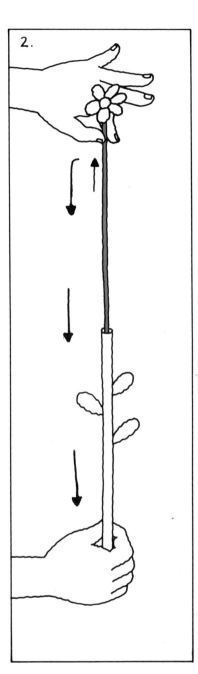

2.

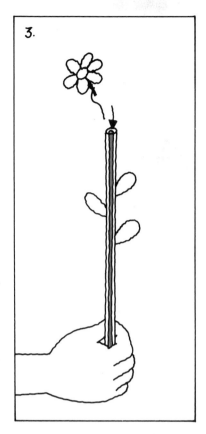

3.

To make this special flower prop, wrap a sheet of green construction paper around a pencil and tape the edges. Slip it off the pencil. Tape a few plastic or cloth leaves to the tube. Tie one end of a cut rubber band to the bottom of a plastic flower. Thread the free end of the band through the paper tube. Then thread the band through the holes of a large button. (The button should be wider than the tube.) Tie a knot to fasten the band to the button.

Pull the flower and band out of the tube and down to the bottom of the stem. Hide the blossom in the hand holding the stem.

Put another flower into the top of the tube. You are now ready to perform the trick.

Cut the rubber band so it is one length. Snip off most of the stem attached to one of the flowers. Tie or staple one end of the rubber strip to the bottom of this flower. (You could make a small loop in the remaining wire and tie the strip to that.)

Slip the other end of the rubber strip through the paper tube. (If it doesn't reach clear through, tie a length of thread to it and draw it through.) Tie this end of the rubber strip to the button. (The button should be wider than the tube.) Be sure the band is tight enough so the flower fits snugly into the top of the stalk when the button is on the bottom. Cut off part of the stem of the second flower so just a short stem is left. You are now ready to practice.

Hold the bottom of the tube in one hand. With the other hand, pull the first flower out of the tube and stretch it (on the band) down to the bottom. Hide the blossom in the hand holding the stem. The rubber strip now runs up inside the tube, then down the outside to the flower hidden in your hand.

Place the second flower into the tube. You will look as if you are holding a stem with a single flower on top.

Pick off the flower and drop it into your pocket. Show your audience the handkerchief, to prove that it is empty, then toss it over the stem. Keep the other flower hidden in your hand.

Ask people to shout several times. On the last shout, toss your hand up so the handkerchief flies off. Release the hidden flower at the same time.

Everyone will be amazed.

tHANK yOu ALL...

48